At the
End of the
Garden

First published in 2007 by
Franklin Watts
338 Euston Road
London
NW1 3BH

Franklin Watts Australia
Level 17/207 Kent Street
Sydney
NSW 2000

A CIP catalogue record for this book is available
from the British Library.

ISBN 978 0 7496 7159 4 (hbk)
ISBN 978 0 7496 7303 1 (pbk)

Series Editor: Jackie Hamley
Editor: Melanie Palmer
Series Advisor: Dr Hilary Minns
Series Designer: Peter Scoulding

Printed in China

Franklin Watts is a division of
Hachette Children's Books.

At the
End of the
Garden

by Penny Dolan

Illustrated by Martin Impey

W

FRANKLIN WATTS
LONDON•SYDNEY

Penny Dolan

"I love the way this friendly scarecrow is so happy, having fun with his friends even on the rainiest of days."

Martin Impey

"I love to paint from my studio at the end of the garden, where Mr Scarecrow Pumpkin-head plays!"

At the end of the garden,
what can you see?

A very funny man by
the old apple tree.

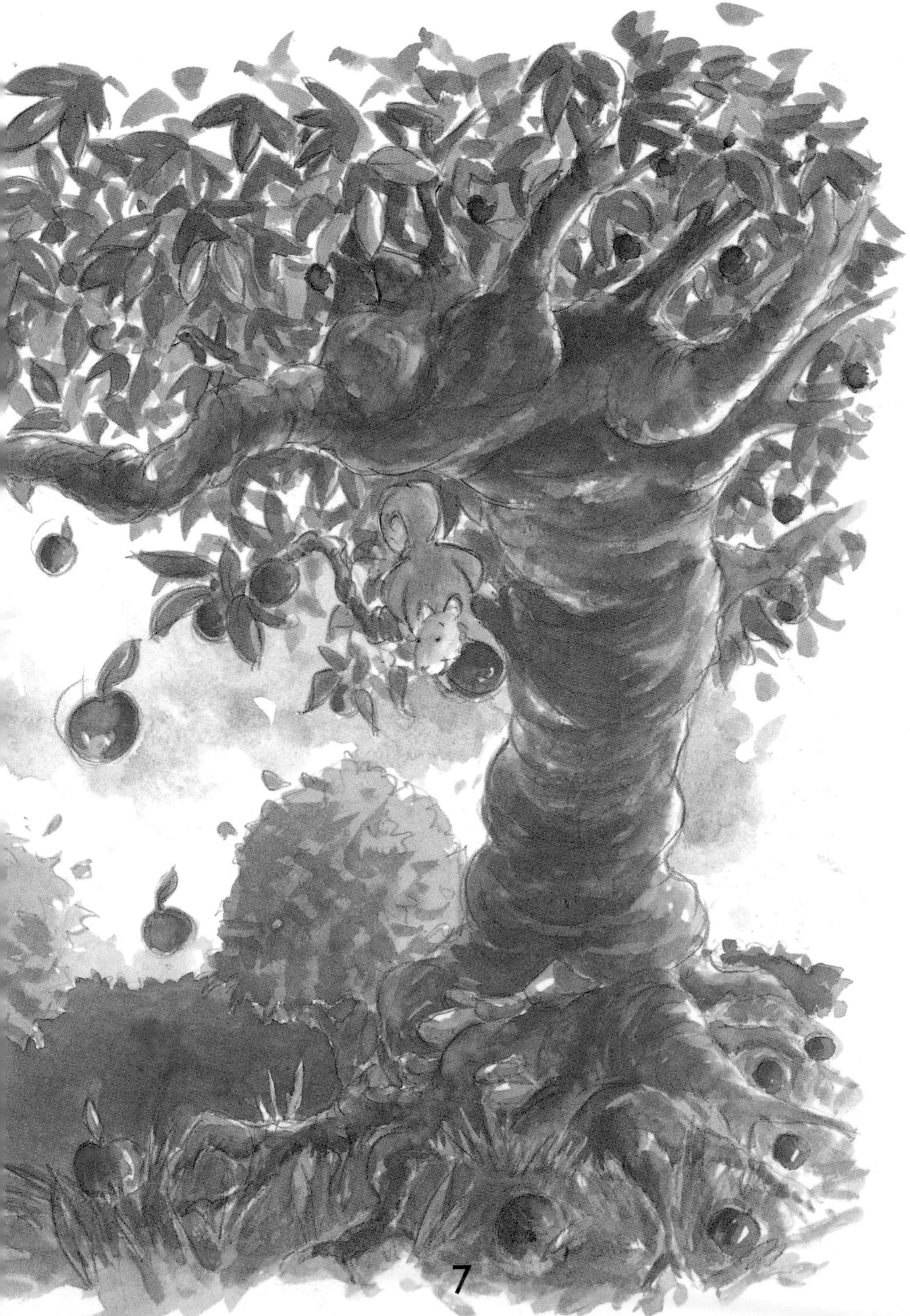

He smiles at the wind.

He smiles at the rain.

He smiles when the
sun comes out again.

11

In his tatty old hat,
there is a robin's nest.

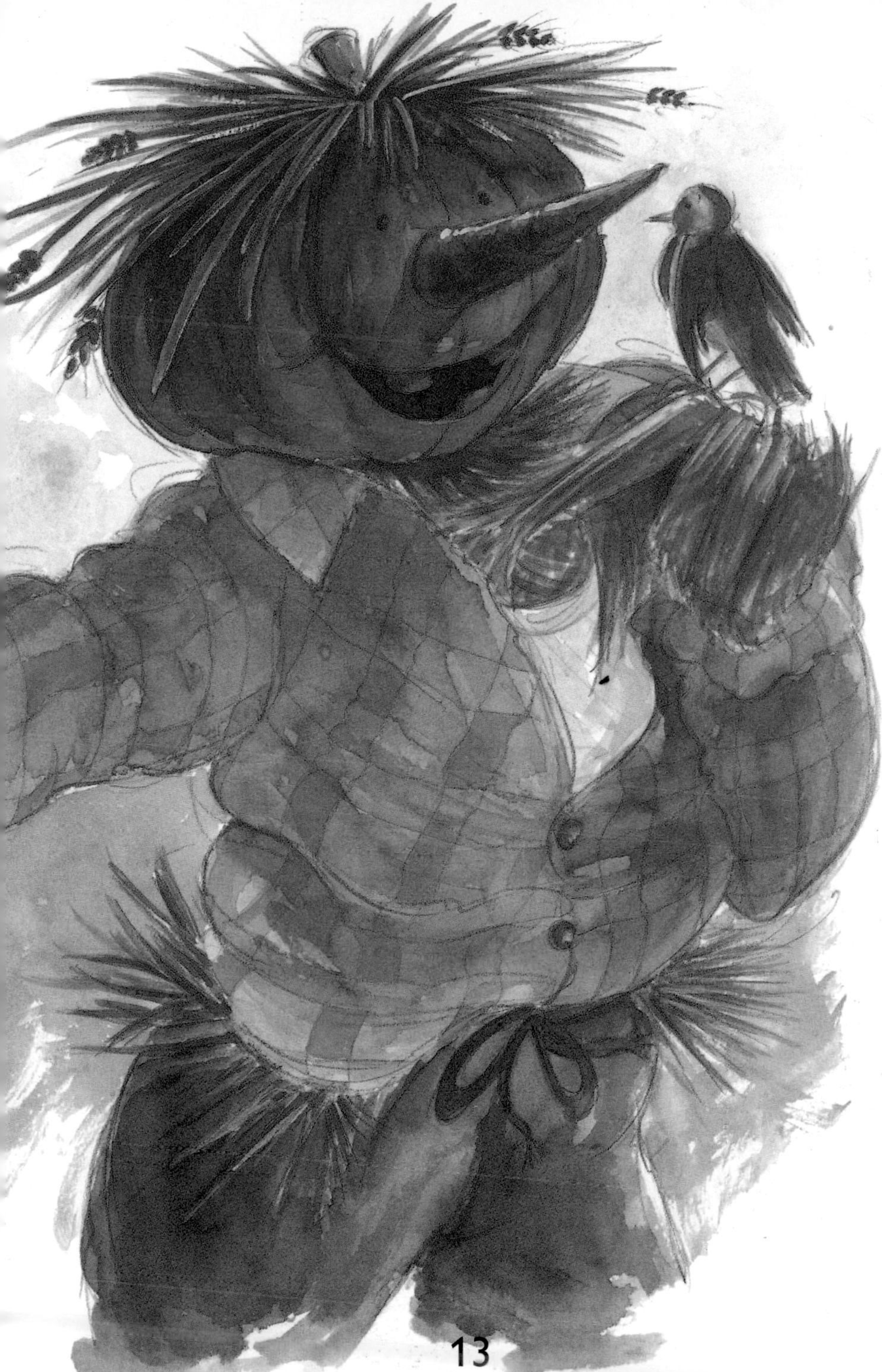

Mice are curled up
in his raggedy vest.

He has beetles
in his boots ...

... and frogs for friends.

19

And he lives way down
where the garden ends.

All year round,
in his earthy bed,

stands Mr Scarecrow
Pumpkin-head.

Notes for adults

TADPOLES are structured to provide support for newly independent readers. The stories may also be used by adults for sharing with young children.

Starting to read alone can be daunting. **TADPOLES** help by providing visual support and repeating words and phrases. These books will both develop confidence and encourage reading and rereading for pleasure.

If you are reading this book with a child, here are a few suggestions:

1. Make reading fun! Choose a time to read when you and the child are relaxed and have time to share the story.

2. Talk about the story before you start reading. Look at the cover and the blurb. What might the story be about? Why might the child like it?

3. Encourage the child to reread the story, and to retell the story in their own words, using the illustrations to remind them what has happened.

4. Discuss the story and see if the child can relate it to their own experience, or perhaps compare it to another story they know.

5. Give praise! Remember that small mistakes need not always be corrected.

If you enjoyed this book, why not try another TADPOLES story?

Sammy's Secret
978 0 7496 6890 7

Stroppy Poppy
978 0 7496 6893 8

I'm Taller Than You!
978 0 7496 6894 5

Leo's New Pet
978 0 7496 6891 4

Mop Top
978 0 7946 6895 2

Charlie and the Castle
978 0 7496 6896 9

Over the Moon!
978 0 7496 6897 6

My Sister is a Witch!
978 0 7496 6898 3

Five Teddy Bears
978 0 7496 7292 8

Little Troll
978 0 7496 7293 5

The Sad Princess
978 0 7496 7294 2

Runny Honey
978 0 7496 7295 9

Dog Knows Best
978 0 7496 7297 3

Sam's Sunflower
978 0 7496 7298 0